D1237521

"This upbeat series really encourages the very young to 'go for it!' with bright vocabulary, illustration and concept . . . These lovely books are true boosters for preschool confidence, self-concept and beginning reading skills."
—*School Library Journal*

Bear can ride his tricycle all by himself, and even his two-wheeler (as long as training wheels are attached to help him balance). But Bear isn't going to stop there. He longs to swoop around gracefully on a skateboard like his older friends. Can he do it? Well, almost.

Children will laugh and cheer as Bear tries harder and harder feats. And they will understand when even dauntless Bear is forced to recognize the limits of his present abilities and has to turn to the use of his imagination.

Sometimes Bear's reach exceeds his grasp, but he knows that it is important to dream big dreams, and to keep trying.

SHIGEO WATANABE'S simple but insightful texts and YASUO OHTOMO'S endearing pictures have made Bear a beloved friend of small children the world over.

I Can Do It All By Myself
books by
Shigeo Watanabe

How do I put it on?
AN AMERICAN LIBRARY ASSOCIATION
NOTABLE CHILDREN'S BOOK

What a good lunch!
Get set! Go!
I'm the king of the castle!
I can ride it!
Where's my daddy?
I can build a house!
I can take a walk!

Text copyright © 1981 by Shigeo Watanabe.
Illustrations copyright © 1981 by Yasuo Ohtomo.
American text copyright © 1982 by Philomel Books.
All rights reserved.
Published in the United States by Philomel Books, a division of
The Putnam Publishing Group, 51 Madison Ave., New York, N.Y. 10010.
Printed in the United States.
Library of Congress CIP information at back of book.

I can ride it!

ory by Shigeo Watanabe   Pictures by Yasuo Ohtomo

SETTING GOALS

PHILOMEL BOOKS

I can ride a tricycle all by myself.

I can ride a two-wheeler, too.

And I can ride a skateboard.

Well, almost.

Now I can do it.

I can roller-skate.

Well, almost.

Now I can do it.

Oops!

I can drive a car.

I can drive a bus.

Can I fly a plane?

Of course I can . . .

. . . someday.

Library of Congress Cataloging in Publication Data
Watanabe, Shigeo, 1928–
I can ride it.
(An I can do it all by myself book; # 5)
Translation from Japanese.
Summary: Not content to ride his tricycle or the
two-wheeler, a bear attempts more difficult feats.
[1. Bears—Fiction. 2. Play—Fiction]
I. Ohtomo, Yasuo, ill. II. Title.
PZ7.W26151c   [E]   81-7792
ISBN 0-399-20867-4   AACR2
ISBN 0-399-61194-0 (lib. bdg.)
ISBN 0-399-21042-3 (pbk)
First paperback edition published in 1985.
Second Impression